Bret Harte

Outcroppings

Being Selections of California Verse

Bret Harte

Outcroppings
Being Selections of California Verse

ISBN/EAN: 9783337275075

Printed in Europe, USA, Canada, Australia, Japan

Cover: Foto ©Andreas Hilbeck / pixelio.de

More available books at **www.hansebooks.com**

BEING

SELECTIONS OF CALIFORNIA VERSE.

SAN FRANCISCO:

A. ROMAN AND COMPANY.

NEW YORK:

W. J. WIDDLETON.

1866.

PREFACE.

IN presenting to the public a volume of this
character, few words of explanation are re-
quired. Its contents have been selected
partly from contributions by local poets to the California newspapers during the past ten years, and
partly from material collected three years ago for a
similar volume, by Miss M. V. TINGLEY.

It might be expected that a country whose scenery
is remarkable for sublimity and grandeur would have
inspired some suitable expression here. But the at-
tempts at descriptive and pastoral poetry have not
been generally successful: perhaps a monotonous cli-
mate, lacking those vicissitudes of seasons which else-
where inspire the imagination, has obliged the poet to

look oftener in his own heart for that Spring and Autumn from which so much imagery is supposed to flow, or in the fortunes of his fellow-men, which are mostly exempt from this climatic influence. It has therefore been thought preferable to select poems relating to a lower plane of incident and experience, as less likely to exhibit a contrast between the subject and its treatment than more ambitious efforts.

For these reasons, some verses have been excluded from this work for which many readers will confidently look, and some admitted which will be equally unexpected. While it is not probable that the rejection or selection of any poem will affect the reputation of the poet, it cannot be denied that the performance of this duty is one attended with some responsibility and peril.

CONTENTS.

—

Edward Pollock.

THE CHANDOS PICTURE.

THE bell far off beats midnight; in the dark
    The sounds have lost their way and wander
      slowly;
Through the dead air, beside me, things cry, " Hark !"
    And whisper words unholy.

A hand, as soft as velvet, taps my cheek;
    These gusts are from the wings of unseen vampires.
How the thick dust on that last tome doth speak
      Its themes,—dead Kings and Empires!

2

This is the chamber;—ruined, waste, forlorn;
Shred of its old-time gilding, paint, and splendor;
And is there none its dim decay to mourn,
In mystic strains and tender?

Why waits no harper gray, with elfin hand
On tuneless chords to harshly hail the stranger—
Who treads the brink of an enchanted strand
In mist, and midnight danger?

I watch, and am not weary; all night long
The stars look shimmering through the yawning
casement;
And the low ring of their unvarying song
I hear without amazement.

How the hours pass!—with that low murmur blent,
That is a part of time, yet thrills us only
When all besides is silent, and close pent
The heart is chilled and lonely.

I watch, and am not weary :—I have heard
  Light steps and whispers pass me, all undaunted:
Have seen pale specters glide, where nothing stirred—
    Because the place is haunted.

And wherefore watch I fearless ? Wherefore come
  These things with windy garments hovering round
    me ?
Whence are the tongues, the tones, the stifled hum,
    That welcomed, and have bound me ?

Lo ! on the wall, in mist and gloom high reared,
  A luminous Face adorns the structure hoary :
Light-bearded, hazel-eyed, and auburn-haired,
    And bright with a strange glory.

'Tis but the semblance of a long dead one—
  A light that shines, and is not ;—clouds are o'er it :
Yet, in the realm of thought, it beams a sun,—
    And stars grow pale before it.

There tend the tones; through that wan atmosphere
   Glide the faint specters with a stately motion;
Slowly, as cloudy ships to sunset steer
      Along the airy ocean.

Shades of the great, but unremembered dead,
   Mourn there, and moaning, ever restless wander;—
For in the presence of that pictured head
      Their waning shapes grow grander.

And here watch I, beneath those eyes sublime,
   A listing to the soft, resounding numbers,
That float like wind along the waves of time,
      And cheat me of my slumbers.

But who shall calm the restless sprites that rove
   In the mute presence of that painted Poet?
In vain their triumph in old wars or love;—
      No future times shall know it.

For, "Oh!" they cry, "his song has named us not!
He stretched no hand to lift the pall flung o'er us."
And still they moan and shriek---" Forgot—forgot!"
In faint and shivering chorus.

Mightiest of all—my master! Dare but I
Touch the shrunk chords thy hand divine hath
shaken,—
How would the heroes of the days gone by
Throng round me, and awaken!

Oh! many a heart the worthiest—many a heart—
Cold now, but once an angel's warm, bright dwelling,
Waits but the minstrel's wizard hand, to start
With life immortal swelling!

And thou, so missed—where art thou? On what
sphere
Of nightless glory hast thou built thine altar?

What shining hosts bow down, thy song to hear—
  Thy heart, the harp and psalter?

Thy dust is mingled with thy native sod:
  Exhaled like dew thy soul, that ranged unbounded:—
But who shall dare to tread where Shakespeare trod,
  Or strike the harp he sounded?

EVENING.

THE air is chill, and the day grows late,
  And the clouds come in through the
    Golden Gate:
Phantom fleets they seem to me,
From a shoreless and unsounded sea;
Their shadowy spars and misty sails,
Unshattered, have weathered a thousand gales:
Slow wheeling, lo! in squadrons gray,
They part, and hasten along the bay;
Each to its anchorage finding way.
Where the hills of Saucelito swell,
Many in gloom may shelter well;
And others—behold—unchallenged pass
By the silent guns of Alcatras:
No greetings of thunder and flame exchange

The armèd isle and the cruisers strange.
Their meteor flags, so widely blown,
Were blazoned in a land unknown;
So, charmed from war, or wind, or tide,
Along the quiet wave they glide.

What bear these ships?—what news, what freight,
Do they bring us through the Golden Gate?
Sad echoes to words in gladness spoken,
And withered hopes to the poor heart-broken:
Oh, how many a venture we
Have rashly sent to the shoreless sea!
How many an hour have you and I,
Sweet friend, in sadness seen go by,
While our eager, longing thoughts were roving
Over the waste, for something loving,
Something rich, and chaste, and kind,
To brighten and bless a lonely mind;
And only waited to behold

Ambition's gems, affection's gold,
Return as "remorse," and "a broken vow,"
In such ships of mist as I see now.

The air is chill, and the day grows late,
And the clouds come in through the Golden Gate,
Freighted with sorrow, heavy with woe;—
But these shapes that cluster, dark and low,
To-morrow shall be all a-glow!
In the blaze of the coming morn these mists,
Whose weight my heart in vain resists,
Will brighten, and shine, and soar to heaven,
In thin white robes, like souls forgiven;
For Heaven is kind, and every thing,
As well as a winter, has a spring.
So, praise to God! who brings the day
That shines our regrets and fears away;
For the blessed morn I can watch and wait,
While the clouds come in through the Golden Gate.

Lyman R. Goodman.

IN THE SWING.

UNDER the apple-blossoms, from the time
    The sun mistook her dimpled cheeks for roses,
And printed sunset kisses upon each,
I swung the farmer's only daughter, Nora.
Oft, as she rose among the purple boughs,
Then, dipping gracefully, swept by me like
A spirit in a dream, the blossoms sent
Such wealth of fragrance after her, I timed
My breathing to the motion of the swing.
And when I told the boyish fancy, Nora—
Shaking the tangled sunbeams from her hair—

Laughed outright, till she would have fallen,
Had I not caught the rope and held it fast.
Sifting a pretext from the circumstance,
I quickly said she must not swing alone.
My meaning fluttered till it lightly touched
Upon an echoing chord within her breast,
And, smiling, she economized the space,
And so made room for both.   And soon. self-swung
By easy art, we swept in airy cycloids—
Each oscillation weaving some new thread
Into the mottled tissue of our talk :
As, who was dead—who married—who. perchance.
Was like to be ; and whether Emma Lyle
Would wed the merchant's or the doctor's son.
Somehow, the subtle thread that tangles hearts—
Blind butterflies !—spun out its golden length
Until it formed the widest stripe of all.
    Nora and I had swung before ofttimes ;
Then, strange—not very strange—to say, our love

Too took a swing, until we quarreled sadly.
The breach had nearly healed,—so far we now
Regarded it as but an episode
Peculiar to love's growth and history.
So, laughing over it, and running on
From this to that,—now angling in the past
For sunny recollections, half forgotten;
Now throwing out our lines into the future
For fair uncertainties; and finally,
Wrapping the present round us, time, and space,
And change,—all but each other,—we forgot.
And when the vesper-light, for lovers lit,
Burned to its socket in the western hills,
The swing had stopped—how long we could not tell,
And vaguely guess;—nor knew we until then
How chill the air was blowing from the sea.
Knitting her hair with crimson blooms, I said:
" May apple-blossoms form the bridal-wreath !"
Then blessing twice and thrice the swing that rocked

The discord of our souls asleep, we parted.
And as her feet, like silver rain-drops, tinkled
Along upon the steps, I faintly heard
Her humming to herself a stanza from
The song I wrote her scarce a year before :—

    " True love is quickened once a year,
        When vernal buds are swelling;
      And warbling tongues are hushed to hear
        The tales their mates are telling:
    The heart that knows no winter's storm
        Can feel no summer's gladness;
    And beauty shows its fairest form
        Smiling through tears of sadness."

Then to my home, and with a sweet " God bless her !"
Fainting upon my lips, I fell asleep.
But still the half-heard melody flowed round
My soul unceasingly, until it grew

Into a radiant form, whose every word
And motion, like itself, seemed music-born;
And in my sinless dreams I worshiped it,
Until it faded in a rosy dawn.

THE BROKEN ROSE.

THE meadow's breath comes cool and sweet;
    A light wind blows
Day's pyre into a purple flame:
A time-worn mound is at my feet,
And on the stone a cherished name,
    And broken rose:

Self-broken from its parent stem,
    While yet the dew
And flush of morn lay on its cheek:
For Love had brought a diadem
As false as falsest tongue can speak —
    A wreath of rue.

You blame her, you who never felt
    The weight that lay
Like heated lead upon her soul,—
The leaden mass that would not melt,
Which death's stern hands alone could roll,
    And lift away.

God holds the key to human hearts;
    We only heed
The surface bubbles, bright and thin,
Or broken, fragmentary parts;
The strange, sealed mystery within
    We cannot read.

Enough for me that Saints conformed
    To mortal molds,
With human imperfections rife.
I loved the grace and virtue, warmed
By Charity, that wrapped her life
    In saintly folds.

I lay my face among the flowers,
    To weep for her:
The violets all whisper—No!
The merle rebukes from leafy bowers,
The lindens, bathed in sunset glow,
    With chidings stir.

All nature cries: " She doth not sleep
    Beneath the sod;
Her feet have left the shores of time,
And now her angel fingers sweep,
Mid swelling anthemings sublime,
    The harp of God."

E. G. Paige.

THE APPROACH OF AUTUMN.

BLOOMING Summer's dead and buried—
    Let the mournful cypress wave;
Sad September now is strewing
    Faded garlands on her grave.
Autumn comes, downcast and lonely;
    Silently she seems to mourn
For the gray hairs in her tresses,
    And her mantle ripped and torn.

In the corner of the door-yard
    Sighs a clump of withered reeds—
Pinks and tulips all have perished,
    And the garden dons its " weeds."

Where the blue-eyed morning-glory
   In its hammock swung on high,
There the yellow-bellied squashes—
   Hang them!—hang themselves to dry.

Golden butter-cups and pansies
   Now no longer gem the field,
While the blossoms that still linger,
   Not a "smell" of perfume yield;
Gaudy dahlias without odor
   With the Autumn days have come.
Stiffly nodding, proudly asking—
   "Stranger, don't you think we're *some?*"

Frogs have ceased their nightly peeping;
   Pollywogs have dropped their tails,
And are grown to great big bullies,
   Croaking in the gloomy vales;

By the pond where hangs the hazel
  Sits a "green-eyed monster" there,
Groaning like a tortured demon,
  In the anguish of despair.

On the pine-top stands a preacher
  Known as Reverend Mr. Crow,
Dressed in black, and preaching patience
  To a hungry flock below;
But in vain the exhortation—
  Rather heed they Nature's laws;
So they leave the lonely Parson,
  Persevering in his *caws*.

Though Pomona glad the market
  With her bounties for the time,
What are apples, pears, and peaches
  To a chap without a dime?—

To a poet, who, like Autumn,
  Goes in very seedy clothes—
Down at mouth and out at elbow—
  Down at heel and out at toes?

Now the day and night are even ;—
  Na'f-an'-a'f, like Johnny's beer;
And Æolus gives his "blow-out"
  At this season of the year.
But the winds will sadly murmur
  When the Equinox is o'er,
And the dead leaves lightly rustle
  Past the woodman's cabin door.

Mournful are thy days, O Autumn,
  Robbing flow'rets of their bloom;
Few, ah, few are left to blossom
  In the shadow of the tomb!

Still Life's pleasures, green as ever,
　　Must not fade and fall till ripe;
So, September, swing thy sickle,
　　While I calmly smoke my pipe!

Emilie Lawson.

BLOSSOM AND FRUIT.

WHY weep for childhood's joys?
  What are they but a round of tricks and
    funning,
  A vast bazar of toys,
And hide-go-seek, and laughs, and cries, and cunning?
  As well grieve for the noise
The brooklet makes, when to the river running!

  When fruit is in its prime,
Who cares for petals dropped in fragrant flutter
  In the sweet blossom-time?—

Or, when the strong man burning thoughts doth
        utter,
    Who sighs for the droll chime
When his queer baby-tongue began to stutter?

    Never doth noonday sigh
To be the dawn again—with crimson flushes!
    No oak-tree towering high
Would be a bush again among the bushes!
    Only weak man doth cry
For babyhood, and nursery tales and hushes!

    Our brightest hours fly fast!
And if we pine for Life's poor frail beginning,
    The golden Now is Past,
While we look backward in regretful sinning:
    Joy waits, and Heaven is vast!
And both are for our seeking and our winning.

And Time is but a school,

Where all great souls to some broad truth awaken;—

A mighty vestibule

Where from our feet the mortal dust is shaken,

And where from ceaseless rule

The hungering, thirsting heart at last is taken.

By Emilie Lawson

WINTERING.

I KNOW of a quaint old farmer,
  More than threescore years and ten,
With a lighter heart and warmer
  Than the most of younger men;
One blithesome and free as the brooklet
  That gurgles through the glen.

He rises at the peep of day
  With the very earliest bird,
And leads his cows to pasture
  With some magical, queer word;
And the scented dew of the clover
  Is first by his brisk feet stirred.

He has a child's complexion,
  Like delicate tinted wax;
But the limbs are rough and hardy
  That shoulder the old ax,
And the hair that drifts o'er his forehead
  Is bleached like the threads of flax.

The young trees fall a-quivering,
  The chip-pile grows anew,
Though he says *he* will never burn them,
  Or, if any, very few;
For he thinks he will never winter
  Another season through.

You may see him in the spring-time,
  When the first young violets peep,
Preparing seed for a harvest
  For other hands to reap;
For he knows the snows of winter
  Will find him fast asleep.

You may find him in the summer-day
  Before the noontide heat,
With birch and spice-wood leaves, and flowers,
  And berries on strings of wheat;
And crowds of children, crazy with joy,
  Dancing around his feet.

Oh, lightsome, happy, happy hours,
  When such a little thing
As strawberries in a birch-bark cup,
  Or raspberries on a string,
Can set the young feet wild with glee,
  And the young heart fluttering.

You may see him in the autumn,
  When the hickory-nuts hail down,
And chestnuts open their burry lips
  And show their teeth of brown,
Gathering herbs for the sick, or nuts
  For the children of the town.

Passing a field of yellow corn
   He will heave a little sigh,
And say he thinks *his* husking-time
   Is very, very nigh,
When the Angel of Death shall take his soul
   And throw the old husk by.

I think you will see this good old man
   Full ten long years from now,
Just ready to go as soon as the hay
   Is gathered in the mow,
Or, at farthest, when the apples
   Are shaken from the bough.

Ever wearing the trusting look
   Of a little child at prayers;
And when the noiseless messenger
   Steals on him unawares,
It will only seem like a toil laid by,
   And a dying away of cares.

PARTING.

THE sun is lying in his western chamber,
 The stately ships are sailing on the bay,
And cloud-hands spread a coverlet of amber,
 Bordered with brown, above the drowsy day:
The opaline skies will shine the same to-morrow,
 And white sails pass gilded with amber light;
But the coming shadow of a parting sorrow
 Shall dim the glory of to-morrow night.

Now, in the West, the radiance grows dimmer,
 The first faint star comes, shining tremulously,
And red rays from the distant light-house glimmer
 Across the foam-capped waters of the sea;

To-morrow's dusk will bring the trembling starlight,
  The wind will chase the white waves to the shore,
And fitfully again will come the far light
  Of warning lamp—but thou wilt come no more.

Ever and everywhere specters of parting
  Stretch forth their weird hands, saddening our mirth:
Ever and everywhere hot tears are starting,
  Where stands the empty chair upon the hearth:
But Nature brightly smiles though hearts are broken,
  Taking at last her children to her breast,
And kindly hides in her mute mounds all token
  Of the great heart-throbs of a life's unrest.

THE LARK AND THE POET.

A YOUNG bird rocked on an apple spray,
  A-trilling a little lay;
Not full-grown was the yellow coat
    Wrapping his slender throat,
And the piping notes had not grown strong,
    But trembled in the song.

A school-boy cried, with thoughtless glee,
    " I will try my skill on thee;"
And the apple-blooms with blood grew red,
    Where the poor heart quivering bled.
Now, sad winds through the branches mourn
    For the song that died unborn.

A poet sat in a solitude,
    Playing a faint prelude—
Snatches of tunes and faltering words,
    And one or two grand chords—
And angel lips to his young ear bent
    As he touched the instrument.

A critic, skilled, and learned, and strong
    (But who never sang a song),
Aimed a cruel arrow carelessly
    As the shy strain floated by;
It brushed the whispering spirit's wing,
It broke the best and finest string,
And sent the young heart sorrowing:
And angel songs, that the poet heard,
    Never found tune or word.

TWO COMRADES IN ARMS.

" COMRADE! I hear the beating of a drum,
    Have re-enforcements come ?"
" There is no sound, save a lost whippowil
    Crying from yonder hill."

" Comrade! I see a spacious mansion stand,
    Built by my grandsire's hand."
" No honored ancestry have left a stone
    That I may call my own."

" Beside its hearth my gentle lady warms
    The sweet child in her arms."
" No tender wife upon her loving breast
    Lulls babes of mine to rest."

" See ! how her bright hair falls in golden showers,
  Twined with autumnal flowers."
" No waving hair, by fragrant flowerets pressed.
  Has my rough hand caressed."

" On what enchanted wings the swift time flies,
  Charmed by those heavenly eyes."
" How dreary, and how long, the sad hours seem !
  Alas ! *I* cannot dream."

" Again I hear the beating of a drum :
  Comrade, has the foe come ?"
" Yes, that great foe—or friend—we all must meet,
  Who never knows defeat."

    *   *   *   *

On the battle-ground, at the break of day.
  Two lifeless soldiers lay;
One face looked pitiful with yearning pain,
  As one who prays in vain;

The other wore a look divinely blest,
  And, from his pulseless breast,
The picture of a lady and a child
  Looked up to him and smiled.

Ina D. Coolbrith.

CUPID KISSED ME.

L OVE and I. one summer day.
    Took a walk together:
Oh, how beautiful the way
    Through the blooming heather!
Far-off bells rang matin-chimes.
    Birds sang, silver-voicing:
And our happy hearts beat time
    To the earth's rejoicing.
Well-a-day! ah. well-a-day!
    Then pale Grief had missed me.
And Mirth and I kept company.
    Ere Cupid kissed me.

Love ran idly where he would,
  Child-like, all unheeding;
I as carelessly pursued
  The pathway he was leading,
Till upon the shadowed side
  Of a cool, swift river,
Where the sunbeams smote the tide
  Goldenly a-quiver:
Well-a-day! ah, well-a-day!
  " Love," I cried, " come, rest thee."
Ah, but Heart and I were gay,
  Ere Cupid kissed me!

Shadows of the summer-cloud
  Fell on near and far land,
Fragrantly the branches bowed
  Every leafy garland;
While, with shining head at rest,
  Next my heart reclining,

Love's white arms, with soft caress,
  Round my neck were twining;
Till—ah, well! ah, well-a-day!
  Love, who *can* resist thee?—
On the river-banks that day,
  Cupid kissed me.

Woe is me! in cheerless plight,
  By the cold, sad river,
Seek I Love, who, taken flight,
  Comes no more forever—
Love, from whom more pain than bliss
  Every heart obtaineth;
For the joy soon vanishes,
  While the pang remaineth.
Well-a-day! ah, well-a-day!
  Would, Love, *I* had missed thee!
Peace and I are twain for aye,
  Since Cupid kissed me!

THE MOTHER'S GRIEF.

SO fair the sun rose, yester-morn,
   The mountain-cliffs adorning!
The golden tassels of the corn
   Danced in the breath of morning;
The cool, clear stream that runs before,
   Such happy words was saying;
And in the open cottage door
   My pretty babe was playing.
Aslant the sill a sunbeam lay—
   I laughed, in careless pleasure,
To see his little hand essay
   To grasp the shining treasure.

To-day no shafts of golden flame
 Across the sill are lying;
To-day I call my baby's name,
 And hear no lisped replying:
To-day—ah, baby mine, to-day—
 God holds thee in His keeping!
And yet I weep, as one pale ray
 Breaks in upon thy sleeping;
I weep to see its shining band
 Reach, with a fond endeavor,
To where the little restless hands
 Are crossed in rest forever!

A LOST DAY.

FROM the shadowy shores of Dreamland,
   In a far and ethereal zone,
I have come unto earth; and I know not
   Where the beautiful Day has flown!

For gazing, at early dawning,
   Where bright in the radiant East
The glittering sun swam, golden,
   Through billows of crimson mist—

My soul floated out on the ether,
   Swift-winged and free as the Light—
Nor ever, till dawn grew to darkness,
   Returned from its airy flight.

I never shall know of its journey:
   I have questioned, all in vain,
The source of the wonderful visions
   That are thronging my puzzled brain.

Strange voices; strange, beautiful faces;
   Strange fashions of mien and dress,
And words whose mystical meaning
   I have striven in vain to guess;

< Strange cities, that mirror the sunlight⌐
  < From minaret, mosque, and dome;>
<And tropical islands, up-springing>
  < From couches of feathery foam—>

All glimmer, and gleam, and glisten,
   Floating on in a magical stream,
Yet shadowed, and vague, and misty
   As the memory of a dream.

And I stand, as at early dawning;
  But where, in the radiant East,
The glittering sun swam, golden,
  Through billows of crimson mist,

There is only this soft, white crescent,
  And the daisy-faced stars, full-blown
In the garden of Night; and I know not
  Where the beautiful Day has flown.

"IN THE POUTS."

CHEEKS of an ominous crimson,
  Eyebrows arched to a frown,
Pretty red lips a-quiver
  With holding their sweetness down;

Glance that is never lifted
  From the hands that, in cruel play,
Are tearing the white rose petals,
  And tossing their hearts away.

Only to think that a whisper,
  An idle, meaningless jest,
Should stir such a world of passion
  In a dear little loving breast.

Yet ever for such light trifles
   Will lover and lass fall out,
And the humblest lad grow haughty,
   And the gentlest maiden pout.

Of course, I must sue for pardon;
   For *what*, I can hardly say!—
But, deaf to opposing reason,
   A woman will have her way.

And when, in despite her frowning,
   The scorn, the grief, and the rue,
.She looks so bewitchingly pretty,
   Why—what can a fellow do?

C. H. Webb.

THE JUNE MONTH.

THE waning of the sweet May moon
   June's laughing face discloses:
Her apron filled with butter-cups,
   Her bosom red with roses.

The blossom and the bursting bud
   Are woven in her tresses;
And every breeze that fans her cheek
   Comes laden with caresses.

The birds all leave the open plains,
   And seek the hazel covers—

Some months were meant for married life,
  But June was made for lovers!

Perhaps you've seen a little maid,
  With lips like rare-ripe cherries?
We're going down the meadow path
  This afternoon—for berries.

I'll tell you more about our walk
  Before the summer closes;
So fill a cup to laughing June,
  And wreathe its brim with roses.

DAS MEERMÄDCHEN.

O H, Spring it is blithe, and Summer is gay :
    The Autumn golden, and Winter gray !

But the seasons come and the seasons go,
All alike to me in their ebb and flow,

Since the day I rode by the cheating sea,
And one of its maidens had speech with me.

Her skin was whiter than words can speak,
The blush of the sea-shell lit her cheek.

Her lips had ripened in coral caves.
And her eyes were blue as the deeper waves.

5

Her long yellow hair fell soft and free,
Like a shower of amber upon the sea.

" Knight! gallant Knight! a boon I pray—
Give me to ride thy charger gray!"

" Oh! ships for the sea, but steeds for the shore—
I'll give thee a boat with a golden oar!"

" Nay, gallant Knight! no charm has the sea—
I would dwell on the green earth ever with thee!"

For her words were fair as her face was fair;
Had she asked my soul, it was hers, I swear!

And I led her, light as sea-birds flit,
Where my steed stood champing his golden bit.

The stirrups of silver were wrought in Spain,
My hand into hers put the silken rein.

And that was the last, though the stars are old,
I saw of my steed with his housings of gold.

Was ever such folly in all the world wide?
But who would have thought a mermaid could ride?

Or a maiden of earth, of air, or the wave,
Should fly from her love with the wings he gave?

Faithless and loveless I walk by the shore—
Never a mermaid has speech with me more.

But this brings not back my charger gray,
Nor the false, false love who rode him away!

THE GOING OF MY BRIDE.

BY the brink of the River our parting was fond,
   But I whispered the words soft and low;
For a band of bright angels was waiting beyond,
   And my bride of a day was to go :

Was to go from our shore, with its headlands of years,
   On a water whose depths were untold;
And the boat was to float on this River of Tears,
   Till it blent with an ocean of gold.

Our farewell was brief as the fall of a tear—
   The minutes like winged spirits flew,
When my bride whispered low that a shallop drew
      near,
   And the beck of the Boatman she knew.

Then I spoke in one kiss all the passion of years,
    For I knew that our parting was nigh;
Yet I saw not the end—I was blinded by tears,
    And a light had gone out from the sky.

But I caught the faint gleam of an outdrifting sail,
    And the dip of a silver-tipped oar;
And I knew by the low rustling sigh of the gale,
    That a spirit had gone from the shore.

All alone in my grief I now sit on the sand,
    Where so often she sat by my side;
And I long for the shallop to come to the strand,
    That again I may sit by my bride.

MY RIVAL.

SOFT music swells out on the night,
   The air is a-throb with perfume,
And the feet of the dancers fall light—
   Yet Death crouches low in the room.

One stands him, all smiling and bland,
   Just there where the tapestries fall;
The wine-cup he holds in his hand
   Throws a dabble of red on the wall.

His fool-face hot flushes with love,
   And he whispers a name in his wine—
The white moon that looked from above
   And the stars know the woman is mine.

It were better he said him a prayer:
    Were the man not a fool, he would feel
A shudder of death in the air,
    And the sharp, sudden tingle of steel.

See! he smiles to himself as he sips
    Of his wine in the alcove apart;
Will he smile when my dagger's thin lips
    Shall drink the red wine of his heart?

UNDER THE STARS.

LOW and dark are the brows of night,
The dews drip dank from the skies—
Warmer than rain, but colder than tears—
Over there where the dead man lies.

Last evening the light of the moon
Floated down like her yellow hair;
And Earth lay asleep, like a bride,
With shoulders uncovered and bare.

But to-night the moonbeams fall,
All shorn of their golden grace,
Like a grave-cloth, white and thin,
Folded over the dead man's face.

Warm and strong is the clasp of love—
  Stronger still is the blow of hate:
Why should one care, when all is paid,
  Whether the reck'ning come early or late!

How it glitters—a sharp-edged knife!
  The stars looked wondering down;
But never a tap of their silver bells
  To waken the slumbering town.

He was pious and good, she said:
  Was it wrong by the churchly code,
When the man was bound for heaven,
  That I helped him along the road?

He was my rival once—
  Whose is the better fate?
He married the girl of his love—
  I murdered the man of my hate!

Charles Warren Stoddard.

AT ANCHOR.

A SAILOR by the green home-shore,
   While seas are ebbing from his view,
  Doth all his early joys renew:
He sings the songs he sang of yore;

He spies his little cot, he smiles
   With a full joy ne'er felt before:
  He holds that one bare prospect more
Than all the Summer of the isles.

The quiet home is his; the trees
   Sprang from the seeds his grandsires laid

Among the mold; within the glade
The myrtles rustle in the breeze,

Above a treasured little grave,
    His early loss, his first deep woe;
    Not any land that he may know
Beyond the purple of the wave

Hath such a jewel in its breast.
    He loves each rock, and stream, and dell;
    'Tis here he only cares to dwell,
'Tis here he ever longs to rest.

This is his home of joy and ease;
    And better is the myrtle tomb
    Than all the heavy dusks that gloom
The groves of spice beyond the seas.

A FANCY.

WHAT would you call the Sun, as he falls
 Out of the heavens, while shadows dim
And rosy are draping the broad sky-walls—
What would you call the Sun, as he falls
 Far down to the ocean's rim?

All of the sky is gathering webs
 Of shadow about it, and the tide—
The lazy tide—as it flows and ebbs,
Is quite entangled with crimson webs,
 And with crimson bloom is dyed.

Perhaps the Sun is an egg of gold
   In a nest of cloud, and Night must be
A fidgety hen—for, look ! she has rolled
Out of the nest the egg of gold,
   And spilled the yelk in the sea !

THROUGH THE SHADOWS.

A LL in a dream i' the twilight,
  Stars glimmer out in their glee;
I hear the low murmur of far-off
  Ripples of tropic sea.

The sorrowful Sun, in the west,
  Is bleeding to death in the wave,
Sraining and tinting with crimson
  The corals that fashion his grave.

Out through the mists and the vapors,
  The cloudy wreaths and the rings,
The sunlight has flown like a butterfly
  Brushing the gold from its wings.

A quiet is coming and folding
  Our troubles away, and our woes
Are hushed in the cool, fragrant shadows,
  Like bees in the heart of a rose.

Come on, little stars, all silver,
  For the terrible Sun has gone,
And forth from the castle of shadows
  The Moon has set sail for the dawn.

Pale are the stars, for the morning
  Is dawning fresh as the May—
So through the shadows we wander forth,
  Seeking the perfect day.

MARS.

NOW Mars steals over the water;
 He is marching down from the sky—
Great Mars, with his golden helmet,
 And the golden flame in his eye.

The sea is still, for the ripples
 Are hushed at the god's slow tread;
And a line of lights is trailing
 The wave, like a burning thread.

Sad Mars! he is wearied with marching
 And wandering off is he,
While he nods his yellow helmet
 And thrusts his lance in the sea.

73

Faltering Mars! with his marching
  Wearied he seems to be;
While he tips his helmet, and merges
  His golden lance in the sea.

6

W. A. Kendall.

TERRAQUEOUS.

[From "ANSTED'S GREAT STONE BOOK."]

FIRST PERIOD.

BARE rocks and vacuous water—
　　Liquid and solid wastes alternate span
Primeval Earth about—
　　No Plant, no Beast, no Man.

SECOND PERIOD.

Cycles of unrecorded time—
Slow transmutations, vast upheavals, shocks:
Dawning of vegetable life—
　　Lichens upon the rocks.

THIRD PERIOD.

Centuries of rain and sunshine—
Fins flash the ocean-depths, the land
Teems with crude animation—
    Brutes wallow on the sand.

FOURTH PERIOD.

More sluggish centuries lapse—
Forests surmount the hills—umbrageous gloom :
Incense exhales and melodies are piped—
    Birds twitter—Flowers bloom.

FIFTH PERIOD.

The age of final preparation wanes—
Declared the consummation of the Plan :
The House is ready—lo, its master comes
    The " Jack of all Trades"—Man!

    *   *   *   *

A link discovered wanting—
A section to complete the circlet human;
The Man is *less* a rib, and straightway finds
    Himself—*plus* Woman!

SIXTH PERIOD.

Generations of masters come and go—
The house absorbs its tenants—all is mystery;
Reason toddles a-pace, babbles, and founds
    Traditional History.

SEVENTH PERIOD.

Inventions and contentions—
Wars, famines, feasts, and plagues;
Prophets and puppets; crucifixions, trinkets—
    Reformers on bow-legs.

———

Not yet the end—perhaps not yet the middle—

Uncertainty its fullness still retains;
Yet, for their derivation—*stone* and *water*—
How wonderful are brains!

MERIDIEM.

FILL once again with wine, the best and last,
    The hour has come the dregs are to be cast—
The regal opulence of Youth is past.

Here let dear memories mingle, as is fit—
The tunes of Song, the genius-gleams of Wit;
The glow of embers ne'er to be relit.

Fill, fill! fill high! Fill to the crystal brim!
And while the sparkling bubble-jewels swim,
Drain to the echo of a dying hymn.

Drain to the murky bottom of the glass—
Drain while the Noon of Life is at high mass—
The shiver of the cups shall cry—" Alas !"

Join in with reckless tongues of hopeless men,
The closing cadence of the grand HAS BEEN—
Ring out this requiem of a Soul's amen !

Oh, for the supple bow for aye unbent !
Oh, for the jocund sense of young content !
Oh, for the star-designs the storms have rent !

Oh, for the passion-second's crimson flight !
Oh, for the moments of supreme delight !
Oh, for the full moon and the honey night !

Oh, for the red, red draught of drunken blisses !
Oh, for the aromatic rapture kisses !
Oh, for the love-blooms and the dream abysses !

Oh, a million times! and all in vain—
The Spring will ne'er return to me again,
With dappled skies and balmy drops of rain.

The lustrous fires that flushed me full of zest,
The amplitude of warmth that overblest,
Have flamed!—and sunk to everlasting rest.

In Indian Summer retrospect I view
The gorgeous hours my wanton luxury slew,
The while their velvet lips were wet with dew—

Dash down the glasses! Let the fragments lay—
Come, penance of exhaustion and decay,
This, this is Pleasure's terrible death-day!

O vanished fragrance of the morning air!
O torrid splendors, lost beyond repair!
The icy night-winds cut me to despair!

And why do I despair? 'Tis that I think
I never more will hear god-glasses clink,
And never more of Nature's blood-wine drink.

But say you, when I'm gone, " His heart was bold ;"
And say you, too, " He was no slave to gold,
And laid no joys away to rust and mold."

Now with the glinting fragments at my back,
I face the Sun upon his paling track,
Declining swiftly into darkness black.

Come others to the revel's vacant seat,
With glasses brimmed, and lips of virgin sweet —
After the carnival we'll fitly greet.

O Spring! O Summer! O unsunned decline!
Sad season of dead thirsts, I now am thine—
At last the Flagon-World is drained of wine!

TRANSITION.

WHEN leaves grow sear, all things take sombre
       hue,
The wild winds waltz no more the wood-side through,
All day the faded grass is wet with dew.

A gauzy nebula films the pensive sky,
The golden bee supinely buzzes by,
In silent flocks the blue-birds southward fly.

The forests' cheeks are crimsoned o'er with shame,
The cynic Frost unlaces every lane,
The ground with scarlet blushes is a-flame!

The one we love grows lustrous-eyed and sad,
With sympathy too thoughtful to be glad,
While all the colors round are running mad.

The sunbeams kiss askant the sombre hill,
The naked woodbine climbs the window-sill,
The breaths the noons exhale are faint and chill.

The ripened nuts drop downward day by day,
Sounding the hollow tocsin of decay,
And bandit squirrels smuggle them away.

Vague sighs and scents pervade the atmosphere. ✂ ✂
Sounds of invisible stirrings hum the ear,
The morning's lash reveals a frozen tear.

The hermit mountains gird themselves with mail,
Mocking the thrashers with an echo-flail,
The while the afternoons grow curt and pale.

84

Inconstant Summer to the tropics flees,
And, as her rose-sails catch the amorous breeze,
Lo! bare brown Autumn trembles to her knees.

The stealthy nights encroach upon the days,
The Earth with sudden whiteness is a-blaze,
And all her paths are lost in crystal maze!

Tread lightly where the dainty violets blew,
Where to Spring winds their soft eyes open flew,
Safely they sleep the churlish Winter through.

Though all Life's portals are indiced with woe,
And frozen pearls are all the world can show,
Feel! Nature's breast is warm beneath the snow.

Look up, dear mourner! still the blue expanse,
Serenely tender, bends to catch thy glance;
Within thy tears sibyllic sunbeams dance!

With blooms full lapped again will smile the land;
The pall is but the folding of His hand,
Anon with fuller glories to expand.

The dumb heart, hid beneath the wintry tree,
Will throb again, and so the torpid bee
Upon the ear will drone his drowsy glee.

So shall the truant blue-birds backward fly;
And all loved things that vanish or that die,
Return to us in some sweet by-and-by.

𝔐.....

TRIAL.

"WHAT! pouting and cross? What is it, love?
  Only a frown, and not a word?"
Pray, had I angered her, or perchance
  The depths of her little being stirred?

Cross, so cross—and a great, dark frown
  There, where the sunshine always lingers;
Spitefully sewing, she doesn't heed
  The needle that pricks her restless fingers.

Pray, can I smooth out the frowns, or bring
  The sunshine back to her face to stay?

Ah! thunder will come to the clearest sky,
    And love can't escape the earthquake day.

Kisses I'll give her—I know they serve
    To smooth out the ruffles in roughest lives;
Kisses will cure all the infant's ills,
    And kisses the little griefs of wives.

So I said: "Come, love, kiss and make up!"
    She stirred, and her passion I thought I'd routed;
"Kiss me!"—she frowned still—"Kiss me, love!"
    Ah! she put up her lips—but only pouted!

TRUST.

MY love is little, but she's very wise,
And sometimes she my little patience tries:
Whene'er she kisses me, she shuts her eyes.

When first I noted it, I, silent, thought,
" 'Tis a new trick my wizard love has caught;
It may not be she shuts her eyes for naught."

And then I said, " What can the reason be?
My love is mine, and few can love as we;
There's naught but love between my love and me."

My self-love whispered, " Here the reason find:
She'd be like Cupid, truest Love when blind.
As she is wise, my winsome love is kind."

Still, not contented,—'twere a pleasure new
If that my love herself would whisper too,
And tell my self-love what it told was true.

And so I said, "My love must make me wise,
And tell me this, which all my wit defies:
Why, when she kisses me, she shuts her eyes."

"You must not ask me." "Nay, love, but I must:
Love is not love without supremest trust.
As you are wise and kind, you will be just."

So, smiling: "Then 'tis, you've so plain a face,
I could not, darling, kiss you else with grace;"
And hid herself, nor blushed at my disgrace.

𝕴. 𝕱. 𝕭owman.

THE LAKE OF THE LILIES.

’TWAS October—bluer, brighter
   Ne’er was sky than o’er us bent;
Through the woods, all gold and crimson,
   Wound the path by which we went;
Till beside the sylvan water
   Where the white pond-lilies float,
Hid by flags and flaunting rushes,
   We espied a tiny boat.

In we stepped: with slender fingers
   Flushing sweetly, laughing low—

Still the gentle echo lingers
   Of that laugh of long ago—
Echo sad that haunts my slumbers,
   Falling faint on brain and ear,
While I listen, wondering, doubting
   If I only dream or hear.

With those slender rose-tipped fingers,
   Boasting all her skill the while.
She adjusted helm and tiller,
   Took the cords with archest smile;
Bade me ply the oar with vigor—
   She the shallop's course would guide.
From the sedge-lined shore we parted—
   Floated o'er the dimpling tide.

Bright the blue sky of October
   Bent above us—gleamed below—
Mirrored in the sylvan water

Where the fragrant lilies grow.
Lost to me the tranquil beauty
  Of smooth lake and arching skies;
I beheld a brighter heaven
  In the depths of azure eyes.

O'er the shallop's side I bent me,
  Plucked the lily floating there;
Bade her note its star-like fashion,
  Bade her taste its fragrance rare.
Beautiful the maiden blushes,
  Which with smiles she strove to hide,
When I said—" These Nature fashions
  For the tresses of a bride."

" Yes," she said, " for raven tresses
  Fairest lilies—purest pearls !"
Then her laughing eyes she lifted—
  Shook her wealth of golden curls,

And a glory seemed to crown her,
   Such as the old masters paint,
In the soft, yet dazzling halo
   Round the brows of pictured saint.

Now our words are low and murmured,
   And the hours unheeded go,
As we drift among the shallows,
   Where the fairest lilies grow.
Now no more her eyes are lifted,
   Paler grows her flushing cheek,
And the tender, pensive silence
   Bids me win her, bids me speak.

And I spoke—in words impassioned --
   All my secret soul revealed,
All the boundless love I cherished,
   Cherished long—so long concealed.
Slowly rose those silken lashes,
   And those clear and candid eyes

Looked in mine serene and tender
  As the depths of April skies.

And that angel head declining
  For an instant seemed to rest,
A beloved and lovely burden,
  On my wildly throbbing breast.
For one brief, ecstatic moment
  Half she sank in my embrace,
While those soft and waving tresses
  Swept my bosom—touched my face.

Floating there among the lilies,
  'Neath October's sapphire sky,
Freely, fondly, then we plighted
  Vows of love that ne'er should die.
Ere in April's sun the snow-wreaths
  Vanished from the mountain's side,
I beheld her at the altar
  Stand a victim—and a bride.

Long in stranger lands I've wandered,
   And no more my feet shall roam
Through the woods—beside the waters
   Of my far New England home;
And its hills and pleasant valleys
   Never more shall glad these eyes,
Dim and weary grown in viewing
   Tropic landscapes—tropic skies.

Long has ocean's waste of waters
   Rolled between my love and me,
And a vaster gulf divides us
   Than the darkest depths of sea.
But in visions sad, yet welcome,
   Oft that autumn landscape gleams.
Oft that gracious presence greets me
   In the moonlight realms of dreams.

THE WHOLE STORY.

WHEN Jones was sixteen, he was bent
On one day being President.

At twenty-five, Jones thought that he
Content as District Judge would be.

At thirty, he was much elated
When Mayor of Frogtown nominated.

But bootless all the nomination—
His rival Tompkins graced the station.

At forty-five, his dreams had fled;
Hope and Ambition, both were dead.

When from his toils he found release,
He died—a Justice of the Peace.

O youthful heart, so high and bold,
Thus is *thy* brief, sad story told!

WAITING.

(AFTER THE GERMAN.)

THE full moon appeareth
  The headland above;
'Tis the hour of meeting—
  Where lingers my love?

The summer night sheddeth
  Its magical spell
O'er forest and ocean,
  O'er mountain and dell.

The summer wind sigheth
  In voluptuous strain;
And my heart is dissolved
  In sweet longing and pain.

The nightingales murmur
  Their loves in soft trills,
And the little leaves shiver
  With passionate thrills.

In earth, air, and ocean,
  Around and above,
Throb the pulses of passion,
  Breathes the music of love.

But hark! 'tis his footstep;
  And soon in his eyes
I shall read the sweet lesson
  Of the earth and the skies.

𝔥. ℭ. 𝔅.

THE OMEN.

BENEATH the mellowing Autumn sky
   We walked the shore, my wife and I:
The tints October's woods that dyed,
The sigh of the retiring tide,
The sun just sinking in the west,
Roused the old longing in her breast—
" Which first shall Death to glory bear?
Which, lonely, weep and wander here?"

Two scallop shells arrest my eye:
" With these will I the omens try;

Conjoined they grew beneath the sea,
Paired and complete and one as we;
That, white and fair, is thine alone;
This, brown and rugged, is my own;
I launch them thus upon the tide,—
Which first shall sink, let Fate decide!"

Thus, half in terror, half in mirth,
I launched the graceful shallops forth.
The wimpling tide retiring bore
Them farther, farther from the shore —
While she pressed closer to my arm,
Hushed breath and heart in sweet alarm:
And cried, as either disappeared,
" Ah, *thine* is gone : 'twas that I feared!"

But still, along the dimpled sea,
Tilted our life-boats buoyantly,
Till, side by side, beyond our sight,

They floated forth into the night.
Then, baffled, awed, rebuked, and still
We stood; and my rebellious will
Felt, mid the hush on sea and shore,
A Presence all unfelt before.

" Forgive, O God! Forgive!" I cried,
" That we have sought what thou dost hide!
Thy secret purpose we would scan,
Distrustful of thy love to man.
Led by thy love our life hath been
By waters still, through pastures green:
Led by thy love our life shall be;
We trust, O God, that life to Thee!"

Carrie Carlton.

THANK GOD FOR RAIN.

THANK God for rain! The parched and thirsty
earth
Lay panting 'neath the glare of cloudless skies:
The sultry air seemed almost luminous with flame,
Save when anon fresh ocean-breezes rise.
Fair Plenty's ruddy form grew strangely thin;
All pinched and shrunken seemed her kindly face,
Till, when men viewed her, with blanched lips they
cried:—
"Gaunt Famine stalketh through our market-place!"

The streams and rivulets had long since died,
Their life too feeble for the sun's fierce ray;

The beasts, and kine, and faithful steed as well,
  Sought vainly for some stream their thirst to stay;
Sweet verdure, that had just sprung into life,
  Grew faint for lack of nourishment, and died.
The young grain, conscious of its own great work,
  Clung feebly to its life, but drooped and sighed.

All men looked vainly for the coming cloud—
  The poor, with what deep prayer God only heard;
But in His ear were poured ten thousand prayers,
  From hearts that never breathed the fearful word—
Famine. " O God, in mercy save !
  Must we thus perish of this awful death ?
In pity send the rain—the blessed rain—
  Or smite us with thy lightning from the earth."

Relenting Heaven smiled on the kneeling earth—
  The scattered clouds in one dark mountain blend—
The cooling winds blow fresh from off the sea,
  And, God be praised ! the gentle rains descend.

" Thank God for rain !" the field and herbage sing :
 " Thank God for rain !" ten thousand souls reply.
O'er all this land rings out a song of praise,
 That to its center shakes the blue-arched sky.

8

Annie A. Fitzgerald.

WAITING FOR THE RAIN.

OH! the Earth is weary waiting,
    Waiting for the rain—
Waiting for the fresh'ning showers,
Wakening all her slumb'ring powers,
With their dewy moisture sating
    Thirsty hill and plain.
Oh! the Earth is weary waiting,
    Waiting for the rain.

Oh! the Earth is weary longing,
    Longing for the rain—

Longing for the cloud-wrapt mountains,
Longing for the leaping fountains,
With their clamorous murmurs thronging
    To the silent plain.
Oh! the Earth is weary longing,
    Longing for the rain.

Oh! the Earth is pained with throbbing,
    Throbbing for the rain—
Pained to see the valley fading—
Pained to see the frost's red braiding
And the with'ring north winds sobbing
    O'er her fields of grain.
Oh! the Earth is pained with throbbing,
    Throbbing for the rain.

Oh! the Earth is sore with sighing,
    Sighing for the rain—
Sighing for the green grass springing,

And the fragrant wild flowers bringing
Beauty—ere the clover dying
    Sear the waiting plain.
Oh! the Earth is sore with sighing,
    Sighing for the rain.

Sore with restlessness and throbbing,
    Throbbing for the rain—
While along the upturned furrow
Busy rooks and blackbirds burrow,
From her wide-spread gardens robbing
    Wealth of scattered grain.
Oh! the Earth is very weary,
    Waiting for the rain.

Waiting restlessly yet weary—
    Waiting for the rain,
For the crystal tear-drops clinging
To the wild oats, fresh upspringing,

And the voices blending cheery'
  With the wild-bird's strain.
Oh! the Earth is sad and weary,
  Waiting for the rain.

And our human hearts grow weary,
  Throbbing day by day—
Thirsting for the fresh'ning showers
O'er the dreams of future hours,
While the present, never sating,
  Glides unfelt away.
Oh! the heart is weary, weary,
  Through its life-long day.

B. P. Avery.

ALONE IN THE WOODS.

FORTH from the busy world rejoiced I come
    To court your influence, ye verdant woods,
Whose templed shades have never caught the hum
    Of odious traffic, nor your solitudes
    Been saddened by the suffering that broods
Like some dark spirit o'er the haunts of men.
    Here, on some hill-top, gazing at the sky,
Or slowly idling through each flowery glen,
    Cooled by the singing brook that ripples by—
My soul can meditate in peace, or smile, or sigh.

Here, while I roam, a thousand centuries seem
  To look on me—poor mortal of an hour!
Yon bounding river, sparkling with a gleam
  Of mid-day light; the granite mounts that tower
  So far above me; and the cliffs that lower
Forever o'er the depths of cañons wild,
  Where savage beings dwell in loneliness,
And mossy bowlders high towards heaven are piled;—
  All these betray a secret mightiness
That makes all human greatness seem but nothing-
  ness.

Here, while I catch the spirit of the scene,
  Rise in my soul traditions of past ages,
Great as the present—but forgot, I ween,
  Save for the art of old historic sages
  Or time-enduring verse of poets' pages;
Majestic empires crumbled to the earth,
  A city's ruins buried 'neath the sea,

With only speculation for their birth;
  Their rise and failure wrapt in mystery
Fathomless as the depths of vast eternity.

Now, like a requiem for grandeur past,
  Floats through my soul some fragment of a song,
Plaintive and low as sounds the piny blast
  When zephyr gently sighs the trees among
  And groweth sadder as he moves along.
Thus Nature wakes to melody the soul
  That woos her charms in solitude retired;
Thus brings the spirit under the control
  Of noble thoughts and yearnings, till 'tis fired
With poesy, and breaks forth in a song inspired.

Thickly around me, piercing to the blue,
  The living columns of the forest stand.
Glimpses of heaven seldom tremble through
  Their verdant capitals, by breezes fanned

And breathing melody, supernal, grand.
No trifling thoughts can start to being here.
　My breath is hushed beneath a solemn spell,
As though I trod in some unearthly sphere:
　My quick heart beats each passing second's knell,
Save when, oppressed, the long-drawn sigh doth from
　　it swell.

In scenes like this blind Ossian raised the note
　Of old, heroic, plaintive northern song,
Whose moving strains to latest times shall float,
　In rich, immortal numbers, wild and strong.
　In scenes like this the spirit goes along
A dim perspective, backward, to the time
　When giant warriors through the forest trod,
Intent on deeds that seemed to them sublime;
　When every grove contained a heathen god,
And mounds o'er slaughtered heroes swelled above
　　the sod.

Lo! here about me, like those mounds of old,
    Are swelling hills—no, billows of the main,
Against the rugged mountains softly rolled,
    But turned to land, and clad with ripening grain,
    Or clover beds, and fragrant blooms whose stain
Was from the rainbow caught, or from the soil
    That hides in stony strata, fathoms deep,
The yellow seeds of wealth: these brawny toil
    Hath come afar to seek, and now each steep
Or gentle hill its beauty can no longer keep.

      *   *   *   *   *

Thou God of Nature! Hadst thou but imbued
    My yearning spirit with the noble gift,
Enjoyed by some, of turning every mood
    The being feels to poetry, I'd lift
    The thoughts of men above mere sordid thrift;
For ah! too much by that mankind are bound,
    Too much of earthiness their course reveals;

Their plodding souls rise seldom from the ground;
   Too seldom tread they o'er the blooming fields,
Courting the purity their beauty freely yields.

But me—a barren shrub fixed in the earth—
   Thou'st blest not with ability to bloom.
Cursed in my later growth as in my birth,
   Unfruitfulness my melancholy doom,
   I pine in solitude and rayless gloom.
Like one in deathly trance, speechless I lie,
   All things perceiving, but expressing naught;
Creation's loveliness enrapt espy,
   My swelling soul with great emotions fraught.
While chill incompetency freezes every thought.

Yet am I thankful *thought* is not *denied*,
   As 'tis to some, unfortunates, who spend
The precious coin of life on joys allied
   To low bestiality; who never wend

With glad yet reverent feet to where ascend
The fanes of Nature in the shady grove.
   Yet am I thankful for the melody
Of morning birds, who, fluttering, sing of love;
   Thankful my heart can throb with sympathy,
And sip from every blossom treasures, like a bee.

THE LONE PINE.

SWAY thy top, thou ancient pine—
  Warrior of the storm commanding!
Lone upon the mountain standing,
Whom no ivy's arms entwine.
Melancholy souls like mine,
  'Neath thy shadow passing slow,
Love to hear thy plaintive moan;
  'Tis an echo of the woe
Found in human breasts alone.

Mournfully amid the ruins
  Of thy fellows standest thou,
Like a column of some temple

Living but in story now;
All around it, wildly scattered,
Fallen walls and pillars shattered.
Softly sighing through thy branches
  Sounds the wind, with fall and swell;
Now retreats, and now advances,
  Rousing fancy with its spell,
Like the melody that chances
  On the ear from distant bell,
Or the murmur that entrances
  Of the tinted sea-side shell.
Lo! musing on thy loneliness,
  Thy brethren seem again to rise:
On every hand a wilderness
  Shuts out the prospect of the skies.

'Tis verdure all, and deepest shade.   No sound
Disturbs the thoughtful silence, save
A murmur such as rolls through ocean cave,

And rustling of dry leaves upon the ground.
But while I listen with an awe profound,
A glance dispels the visionary wood—
A single tree remains where late ten thousand stood.

L. F. Wells.

TOM DARLING.

TOM Darling was a darling Tom
  (Excuse all vulgar puns);
A type of California's bright
  Rising and setting sons.

His father was an austere man—
  An oyster-man was he,
Who opened life by opening
  The shell-fish of the sea;

But hearing of a richer clime,
  He took his only son,
And came where golden minds are lost.
  While golden mines are won.

They hoped to fill their pockets from
  Rich pockets in the ground:
And midst the bowlders of the hills
  None bolder could be found.

For though a mining minor. Tom
  Was never known to shirk:
And while with zeal he worked his claim.
  His father claimed his work.

Time's record on his brow now showed
  A fair and spotless page:
And, as his age became him well,
  He soon became of age.

9

Thinking that he was up to all
  The California tricks,
He now resolved to pick his way
  Without the aid of picks.

In less than eighteen circling moons
  Two fortunes he had made;
One by good luck at trade in stock,
  And one by stock in trade.

With health and wealth he now could live
  Upon the easy plan;
While everybody said, of course,
  He was a fine young man.

But Thomas fell, and sadly too—
  Who of his friends would 'thought it?
He ran for office, and, alas
  For him and his!—he caught it.

Mixing no more with sober men,
  He found his morals fleeing;
And being of a jovial turn,
  He turned a jovial being.

With Governor and Constable
  His cash he freely spends;
From Constable to Governor
  He had a host of friends.

But soon he found he could not take,
  As his old father would,
A little spirits, just enough
  To do his spirits good.

In councils with the patriots
  Upon affairs of State,
Setting no bars to drinking, he
  Soon lost his upright gait.

His brandy straightway made him walk
   In very crooked ways;
While lager-beer brought to his view
   A bier and span of grays.

The nips kept nipping at his purse—
   (Two bits for every dram)—
While clear champagne produced in him
   A pain that was no sham.

His cups of wine were followed by
   The doctor's painful cup;
Each morning found him getting low
   As he was getting up.

Thus uselessly and feebly did
   His short existence flit,
Till in a drunken fight he fell
   Into a drunken fit.

The doctors came, but here their skill
   They found of no avail;
They all agreed, what ailed poor Tom
   Was politics—and ale.

MARY BROWN.

SHE dwelt where long the wintry showers
    Hold undisputed sway,
Where frowning April drives the flowers
    Far down the lane of May.
A simple, rustic child of song,
    Reared in a chilling zone,
The idol of a household throng—
    The cherished one of home.
None sang her praise, or heard her fame
    Beyond her native town;
She bore no fancy-woven name,
    'Twas simply Mary Brown.

Her eyes were not a shining black,
    Nor yet a heavenly blue,
They might be hazel, or, alack!
    Some less poetic hue;
Indeed, I mind me, long ago,
    One pleasant summer day,
A passing stranger caught their glow,
    I think he called them gray.
Yet when with earnestness they burned
    Till other eyes grew dim,
Their outward tint was ne'er discerned—
    The spell was from within.

A novelist, with Fancy's pen,
    Would scarcely strive to trace
From her a fairy heroine
    Of matchless mien and grace—
A model for the painter's skill,
    Or for the sculptor's art,

Her form might not be called; yet still
  It bore a gentle heart;
The while it fondly treasured long
  Love's lightest whispered tone,
In other hearts she sought no wrong—
  She knew none in her own.

Though never skilled in Fashion's school,
  To sweep the trembling keys,
Or strike the harp by studied rule,
  A listening throng to please:
Yet still, when anguish rent the soul,
  And fever racked the brain,
Her fingers knew that skillful touch
  Which soothed the brow of pain—
And widow thanks, and orphan tears
  Had owned her tender care,
While little children gathered near,
  Her earnest love to share.

I might forget the queenly dame
  Of high and courtly birth,
Descending from an ancient name
  Among the sons of earth:
I scarce recall the dazzling eyes
  Of her, the village belle,
Who caused so many rural sighs
  From rustic hearts to swell:
Yet never can I cease to own,
  While future years shall roll,
Thy passing beauty, Mary Brown—
  The beauty of the soul.

 Mrs. A. M. Shultz.

THE SONG OF THE FLUME.

AWAKE, awake! for the flaming east
   Is red with the coming day;
My struggling breast disdains its rest,
   And I haste o'er the hills away.
Up from the valley!—up from the plain!
   Up from the river's side!
For I come with a gush, and a torrent's rush,
   And there's wealth in my swelling tide.

I am fed by the melting rills that start
   Where the sparkling snow-peaks gleam;

My course is free, and with greatest glee
   I leap in the sun's broad beam.
Though torn from the channels deep and old
   I have worn through the craggy hill,
Yet I flow in pride as my waters glide,
   And there's mirth in my music still.

I sought the shore of the sounding sea
   From the far Sierra's hight,
With a starry breast and a snow-capped crest,
   I foamed in a path of light;
But they bore me thence in a winding way—
   They fettered me like a slave,
And as serfs of old were sold for gold,
   So they bartered my soil-stained wave.

Through the dim tunnel, down the dark shaft,
   Search for the shining ore;
Hoist it away to the light of day

Which it never has seen before!
Spade and shovel, mattcck and pick—
   Ply them with eager haste;
For my golden shower is sold by the hour,
   And the drops are too dear to waste.

Lift me aloft to the mountain brow!
   Fathom the deep blue vein!
And I'll sift the soil for the shining spoil,
   As I sink to the valley again;
The swell of my swarthy breast shall bear
   Pebble and rock away,
Though they brave my strength, they shall yield
      at length,
   But the glittering gold shall stay.

Mine is no stern and warrior march,
   Nor stormy trump and drum;
No banners gleam in my darkened stream,

As with conquering step I come;
But I touch the tributary earth
Till it owns a monarch's sway,
And with eager hand, from a conquered land,
I bear its wealth away.

Awake! awake!—there are loving hearts
In the land you left afar;
There are tearful eyes in the homes you prize.
As they gaze on the western star.
Then up from the valley!—up from the hill!—
Up from the river's side!
For I come with a gush and a torrent's rush.
And there's wealth in my swelling tide!

J. R. Ridge.

ERINNA.[1]

IMAGINATION! rouse thee from repose,
    And to our eyes Erinna lost disclose;
Since, from the living voice of time is gone
Her genius-gifted and melodious tone,
And from his star-lit page the words are fled
She from her early lyre in wonder shed!
Arouse thee! fling around her fancied form
A glorious hue—a beauty rich and warm.

---

[1] Erinna, a native of Lesbos, and friend of Sappho, died at the early age
of nineteen. She is described as a girl of extraordinary beauty and genius;
but her works, all except two or three epigrams, have unfortunately perished.
—*Poets and Poetry of the Ancients,* by WILLIAM PETER, A. M.

'Tis done: alone, by Lesbos' wave-washed strand,
I see her in the pride of beauty stand,
Far gazing where the Ægean waters smile
Around her native home and classic isle.
Soft blow the breezes on her snowy brow,
And stir the folds around her limbs that flow;
Her golden hair's luxuriance on her neck
Falls unregarded down; it needs no check—
For who would comb the plumage of the bird,
Or smooth the dimpling waves by Zephyr stirred?
Her small white hands are linked beneath her zone,
And 'tween her sweetly rounded arms are shown
Twin spheres of Love, and Pleasure's burning throne!
A glow is on her cheeks, and fresh her lips
As evening cloud the Sun's vermilion tips;
Her clear bright eye wild wanders o'er the main,
That, rolling its blue waves along, a strain
Eternal utters, and sublime, to charm
The fair green isles that o'er its bosom swarm.

Ah! beautiful indeed!   What magic gives
The grace that in her every movement lives?
What power, unseen, is breathing o'er her face,
Where every lineament divine we trace?
It is the magic Sorcerer, never stole
From Science dread—the magic of the Soul!
It is the power of genius Heaven-conferred,
Which, voiceless though it be, and aye unheard,
Imparts its own true beauty to the face,
And lends unto the form its bloom and grace.

Erinna! mid the objects Time has cast
His hand upon, thou stand'st within the past
In lonely and peculiar loveliness!
The child of song, with Nature's own impress
Upon thee—yet thy harp is hushed, and no
Sweet strains of thine through distant times shall flow;
Thy voice has perished, sweetly though it sung,
And perished those who on its accents hung;

Thou wert a bird, that breathed its soul away
In song, and died—but Echo lost the lay;
Thou wert a star, which shone a single night,
And set, to bring no more its worshipped light.
Thou *art* a glorious image of the mind,
Seen through the depths of ages, far behind,
Round which our fancy flings her brightest beams.
While ancient story faintly aids her dreams.
The friend of Sappho—linked together be
Those names, and never wrecked on Time's wide sea:
And when we read the passion-wildering strain.
Of Sappho's muse, that charms the listening brain.
We'll feel Erinna's voice our hearts inspire,
And dream *her* lovely hand is on the lyre.

10

J. C. Duncan.

THE INTAGLIO.

LINES ON A BEAUTIFUL ANTIQUE.

ON the temple-crownèd summit,
  O'er the waters of the bay,
Lingered yet the rosy sunlight,
  Lingered yet the dying day!

O'er the Pantheon's sculptured beauties
  Light and shade were playing still,
Matchless statues, life-like tinted,
  Stood upon Minerva's hill.

Gazing on his work completed,
  Carved upon a sparkling stone,

Sat an artist in the twilight,
  Like a monarch on his throne!

And his subjects were around him,
  Called forth by a master's power—
Genius, with its bright creations,
  Peopled there the passing hour.

But a face of rarer beauty
  On his dreams had never shone,
Than the one his hand had graven
  Deep within the gem-lit stone.

From the Past that face was chosen!
  There its gaze still seemed to be—
Flashing by the dying sunlight
  Shone the word Mnemosyne!

Full two thousand years their changes
  Mark upon the sculptured wall;

Ruins, mighty in their ruin,
  Spread o'er Greece a nation's pall!

Full two thousand years are numbered
  Since that artist's task was done—
Since in glory Athens sparkled,
  Lit up by that setting sun.

Yet the carvèd gem remaining
  Tells us of that golden age,
And bids Memory's face restore us
  Light to read her brightest page.

 ❋   ❋   ❋   ❋   ❋

On the temple-crownèd summit
  Breaks again the rising day,
Streaming with its dawning brightness
  Down the waters of the bay!

See, the centuried mist is breaking!
  Lo, the free Hellenic shore!

Marathon—Platæa tell us
   Greece is living Greece once more.

O'er the island-gemmed Ægean,
   By the zephyr borne along,
List the muse of plaintive Sappho—
   Hear Anacreon's wine-pressed song.

Stately temples stand before us,
   Where the wisest masters taught—
Fairest in their fair proportions,
   Columned halls where Phidias wrought.

Hark! a voice from the Agora
   Bids a thousand voices cease—
Pericles, the lord of language,
   Stirs to war, or soothes to peace!

Painting, by her rival sisters,
   Stands in her meridian day;

Rivaling Nature by her semblance,
  Bidding Nature homage pay![1]

See those gilded letters glowing—
  Mark that laurel wreath of fame—
Æschylus, they give *thy* verses:
  Sophocles, they wreathe *thy* name!

*   *   *   *

Lo, the mist again is closing
  O'er the waters of the bay—
Night, her mantle now enfolds it:
  When will come again the day?

Full two thousand years are numbered
  Since that artist's task was done—
Since in glory Athens faded,
  Lit up by that setting sun!

The birds, it is said, plucked at the painted fruit exhibited by an artist in the market-place of Athens.

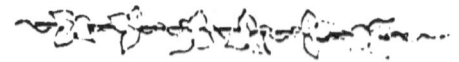

James Linen.

I FEEL I'M GROWING AULD.

I FEEL I'm growing auld, gude-wife,
   I feel I'm growing auld;
My steps are frail, my een are bleared,
   My pow is unco bauld.
I've seen the snaws o' fourscore years
   O'er hill and meadow fa',
And, hinnie! were it no for you,
   I'd gladly slip awa'.

I feel I'm growing auld, gude-wife,
   I feel I'm growing auld;
Frae youth to age I've keepit warm
   The love that ne'er turned cauld.

I canna bear the dreary thocht
   That we maun sindered be;
There's naething binds my poor auld heart
   To earth, gude-wife, but thee.

I feel I'm growing auld, gude-wife,
   I feel I'm growing auld;
Life seems to me a wintry waste—
   The very sun feels cauld.
For lang, lang years ye've been to me
   O' warldly friens the best;
Now, I'll lay down my weary head,
   Gude-wife, and be at rest.

www.ingramcontent.com/pod-product-compliance
Lightning Source LLC
Chambersburg PA
CBHW031121020726
47495CB00007B/2301